Padraic Pearse

Three Lectures on Gaelic Topics

Padraic Pearse

Three Lectures on Gaelic Topics

ISBN/EAN: 9783743407282

Manufactured in Europe, USA, Canada, Australia, Japa

Cover: Foto ©Andreas Hilbeck / pixelio.de

Manufactured and distributed by brebook publishing software
(www.brebook.com)

Padraic Pearse

Three Lectures on Gaelic Topics

Three Lectures

ON

Gaelic Topics

BY

P. H. PEARSE

President of the New Ireland Literary Society

𝔇ublin

M. H. GILL AND SON

———

1898

M. H. Gill & Son, Publishers, Dublin

To the

VICE–PRESIDENT AND MEMBERS

OF THE

NEW IRELAND LITERARY SOCIETY,

THIS LITTLE VOLUME IS INSCRIBED

BY THEIR

PRESIDENT

PREFACE

HE three lectures or papers comprised in this little volume were not originally intended to see the light of publication. They were written, in every case, at a few days' notice, and at different periods during the last twelve months. Though I have revised them for publication, yet I have not, by any means, made so many emendations as I would like, preferring to send them forth as nearly as possible in their original forms.

I hope no one will be so uncharitable as to imagine that I have published this booklet merely for the sake of seeing myself in print. My main object as a matter of fact has been to assist, in some little degree, in spreading the reputation of the Society of which I have the honour to be President, and before which the lectures were delivered.

As I am but a student of Irish myself—and young at that—I am aware that Gaelic scholars will find little that is new in these papers ; but it is not so much to the scholar they are addressed as to the barbarian—to him, that is, to whom our National language, with its wealth of poetry, romance, and folk-lore, is still a sealed book. The subjects of which the lectures treat are to-day far from being so new, or so out-of-the-way, as they would have been even a very few years ago ; for, thanks to the Gaelic League, to the *Oireachtas*, to the *Gaelic Journal*, and to "Ράιnne an Lαe," Irishmen are beginning to realize that they possess a language of their own, which, for antiquity, may vie with the languages of Homer and Virgil, and, for youthful vigour and literary capabilities, with the languages of Dante, Shakespeare, and Goethe.

CONTENTS

I.—GAELIC PROSE LITERATURE *

A GREAT deal, Mr. Chairman, has, within the last few years, been said and written about the ancient literature of the Gael. In Ireland, in Great Britain, and on the Continent, a small but earnest band of workers is engaged in opening up to the world the vast literary treasures of the Irish language. In spite of this, however, the melancholy fact remains, that, to most people, our literature—prose and poetry—is still a *terra incognita ;* a region as dark and unexplored as the heart of Africa. Hence, as might naturally be expected, we constantly find two very different opinions expressed by two very different classes of people. First, we have the assertion of ignorant and self-important critics of the "up-to-date" school, that the literature existing in the Gaelic language is of an utterly worthless type—that it consists of a few odd songs written by disreputable and half-educated poets, and of certain crazy old tales

---

* Read in March, '97.

about Fenians, giants, reptiles, and soforth. On the other hand, we have the far more pardon-able and far less erroneous belief of enthusiastic Gaelic students, that the Irish language possesses the grandest, the most ancient, and the most extensive literature in the world. Now, the truth of the matter is simply this : there are, at the present day, several nations possessing a literature more extensive, and possibly of a higher *absolute*, though certainly not of a higher *relative*, degree of excellence, than Gaelic litera-ture ; but the statement is strictly and undeni-ably true that Ireland possesses a more ancient, a more extensive, and a better literature, *wholly of native growth*, than any other European country, with the single exception of Greece.

It is impossible, of course, to determine the precise date at which our forefathers first com-menced to commit tales and poems to writing. We know that they possessed *some* books, at least, before the arrival of St: Patrick ; but it is highly probable that these were derived either from St. Patrick's predecessors in Ireland, or from communication, commercial or otherwise, with the Christians of the Continent.   It is true that many of our existing romances are, in incidents and tone, completely pagan; that these existed, in some shape or other, long before the time of St. Patrick is absolutely certain ; that they existed in a written form is, at least, possible.   We may conclude, then, that Irish literature, using " literature " in the strict sense of the word, dates from the fourth or fifth century of the Christian era.

The way in which our early literature was produced and propagated is a remarkable one. Handed down by word of mouth for centuries, it was at length committed to writing—sometimes by the professional bards themselves, more frequently, perhaps, by the humbler scribes, lay and ecclesiastical. The service rendered to Gaelic literature by these latter is indeed immense : in the quiet shelter of great monastic establishments, or under the friendly protection of powerful chiefs, these old Gaelic scribes lived and died ; their cunning pens it was that illuminated the pages of our priceless manuscript-books, and that gave to the world the vast stores of Gaelic literature, which, having survived the ravages of Dane, and Norman, and Cromwellian, are scattered to-day through the libraries of Europe, from the Liffey to the Tiber, from the Tiber to the Neva.

Eire has long been celebrated as the " Land of Song." It is hence somewhat remarkable to find that prose has played a more important part in the early literature of Ireland than in that of any other country. Our great national epics—including, of course, the *Táin Bó Cuailgne*, which is recognized as emphatically *the* national epic—are all in prose.* There exists, then, in the Irish language, a most valuable, a most extensive, and a most unique prose literature. It is in this *uniqueness*, indeed, that the chief charm of Gaelic prose lies. There is absolutely nothing like it in the world's literature. When the student enters its wide realms he finds himself in a new world, surrounded by a new atmosphere, new characters, new incidents, new modes of thought. The nearest approach to our older romance-literature is perhaps to be found in those splendid old sagas of the Nordland, which are lately becoming so popular

---

* It is probable, however, that they were *originally* in poetry.

amongst English scholars. It is well known, indeed, that some of the Scandinavian epics are directly borrowed from our Gaelic epics—style, characters, incidents, and all.

Speaking very broadly, Gaelic prose may be divided into two great chronological divisions. The former, extending up to the sixteenth century, a period of over a thousand years, was the reign of the bards—and a long, glorious and prolific reign it was ; the latter, which includes the last three centuries, is a period of decline, fall, and finally, of resurrection.

The former of these two divisions should properly be sub-divided into two, ancient and mediæval. The former would embrace a period extending from the fifth century to the twelfth the latter from the twelfth to the sixteenth. The prose styles of these two periods are very different: that of the former is severe, unadorned, unencumbered by unnecessary words ; the latter, on the contrary, is marked by a ponderous, ornate, multi-adjectival style, often extremely interesting, but sometimes degenerating into bombast.

For the purposes of this lecture I shall consider these two divisions as one, the later being, as a matter of fact, merely the developed form of the earlier.

It is to this period then—the reign of the bards, as I call it—that I shall almost entirely confine my attention. The amount of literature which was produced during this thousand years or so is simply incredible ; by far the greater part of it has perished, but there still remains enough to fill some 1,400 printed volumes, and to keep the Celtic scholars of Europe busied in editing and publishing it for the next two centuries. Yet, in the face of these facts, we frequently hear educated Irishmen assert that the Irish language has produced no literature! "*O tempora! O Mores!*"

This enormous mass of prose may again be sub-divided into numerous classes: history, biography, historic-romance, and fiction, or romance undiluted. The first of these divisions, however, can scarcely come under the head of "literature," being, for the most part, mere annals, or compilations of dates and facts; the second, that of biography, is mostly of a hagiological kind: it deals, that is, with the lives ot the early Irish saints, and though most valuable and interesting in itself, and frequently of a high degree of literary excellence, it has not the claims to popularity amongst general readers that the latter two classes have.

We now come to the romantic prose literature of Ireland, part of it a mixture of genuine history and fiction, much of it, no doubt, fiction pure and simple. There is no literary production of any age or nation so entrancing, and, if I might use the word, so *refreshing*, so *bracing*, as these romantic prose-works; they have an atmosphere of old-world quaintness and freshness about them, they are pervaded by a poetic magic and glamour peculiarly their own; the poet, or the scholar, or the antiquarian, finds in them a wealth of beauty, of imagination, of historic lore, which he can find nowhere else. Yet, in spite of all this, there is almost a universal opinion—which exists even amongst lovers of the language—that Gaelic romantic prose is of the driest and most uninteresting character. How this absurd misconception has grown up, and holds ground, I am positively unable to conceive—unless, indeed, it be due to the nature of the works generally selected as text-books, or to the bad and unreadable translations which editors of such works conceive themselves bound to make.*

Our historic-romantic literature deals with many personages and events, but the larger part of it can be grouped into three great cycles : the mythological cycle, the early heroic cycle (which centres round Cúchulainn and the knights of the Craobh Ruadh), and the later heroic cycle (which circles round Fionn, the son of Cumhal, and the Fianna Eireann). Some of the tales, at least as we have them at present, are mere fragments ; most of them, however, are sagas of considerable, indeed, sometimes of almost appalling length. In the later romances we find the very first examples of that form of literature which exerts such a potent influence to-day— the novel. The *Toruigheacht Dhiarmuda agus Ghráinne*, is neither more nor less than a novel —a novel with a regular and most artfully-contrived, yet perfectly natural, plot. It is, as a matter of fact, one of the greatest and one of most interesting historical novels ever written.

Of the three cycles, the mythological is, of course, the oldest ; whilst the second or Red-Branch cycle is the finest from a literary point of view. As the three, however, as far as style and incidents are concerned, are perfectly similar,

---

* Absolutely the best living translator of romantic Gaelic prose is Rev. Dr. Hogan, S.J. His translation of *Cath Rois na Riogh* is scholarly, accurate, and withal a splendid piece of English prose. The fault of most translations from the Gaelic is that they are too literal ; the spirit of a work *cannot* be preserved in a word-for-word translation. Who would think of putting into the hands of a student a word-for-word translation of, say, a Greek or Latin classic, or of a modern French or German work ?

it will be sufficient for me to make a few general remarks on their character, illustrating by one or two extracts.

The first point that strikes the reader of Gaelic prose, and particularly of this special kind, is its wonderful descriptive power. Irish, from its copiousness and expressiveness, is, perhaps, better adapted for description than any other language. It is especially rich in beautiful and sonorous epithets, and many of these are so delicately shaded in meaning that, though their signification and application are perfectly clear in Irish, yet they must frequently be rendered by the same word in English.* It is by piling up such epithets as these that the really marvellous descriptive effect I have alluded to is obtained.

There are two scenes in the description of which our old storytellers particularly excel, and they are constantly recurring in our romantic literature—a battle and a sea-voyage. To select the most suitable specimen of a battle piece where there is so large a field of choice is somewhat difficult. I shall begin, however, with the *Táin Bó Cuailgne* itself—one of the oldest, and certainly the finest and most important of the epic-romances of the Red-Branch cycle. Here is Sullivan's translation of a portion of the "Fight at the Ford" between Cúchluainn and his friend Ferdiad:—

"So close was the fight they made now that their heads met above and their feet below and their arms in the middle over the rims and bosses

---

* There are many Irish words which absolutely defy translation into English : Miss Norma Borthwick ("Ccoᵬ Ruaᵬ,") in her prize essay in Gaelic at the recent Oireachtas instances, amongst others, "plaiᴄeaṁail," and "ᴄráiᴄnín."

of their shields.   So close was the fight they
made that they cleft and loosened their shields from
their rims to their centres.   So close was the fight
which they made that they turned and bent and
shivered their spears from their joints to their hafts !
Such was the closeness of the fight which they
made that the Bocanachs and Bananachs and wild
people of the glens and demons of the air screamed
from the rims of their shields, and from the hilts of
their swords, and from the hafts of their spears.
Such was the closeness of the fight which they made
that they cast the river out of its bed and out of its
course, so that it might have been a reclining and
reposing couch for a king or for a queen in the
middle of the ford, so that there was not a drop of
water in it unless it dropped into it by the tramp-
ling and the hewing which the two champions and
the two heroes made in the middle of the ford.
Such was the intensity of the fight which they made,
that the stud of the Gaels darted away in fright
and shyness, with fury and madness, breaking their
chains and their yokes, their ropes and their traces,
and that the women and youths and small people
and camp-followers, and non-combatants of the men
of Eire broke out of the camp southwestwards."

Here is another description of a single fight
translated by Father Hogan from the *Cath
Rois na Riogh*, or "Battle of Rosnaree."   This
battle was fought on the Boyne about the first
year of the Christian era, and the saga describing it is, both in its older and more modern
forms, quite pre-Christian in tone and texture.
Cúchulainn had been inflicting heavy slaughter
on the men of Leinster, or, as a Gaelic bard
would put it in euphemistic-poetic language, *he
had been playing the music of his sword on them*,
when he approached the ring of battle in which
he saw the diadem of the high-king, Cairbre Nia
Fear himself : after an interchange of defiances

" Those two smote each other, and each of them

inflicted abundance of wounds on his opponent, and they plied furious, angry, truly grim, effort-strong strife against each other, and they quickened hands to smite fiercely and feet to hold firm against the encome of the fight and of mutual wounding. Howbeit, stout were the strokes and fierce the live-wounds, strong were the good thrusts, earnest was the hard fighting, and stern were the hearts, for it was a smiting of two brave champions, it was a lacerating of two lions, it was a madness of two bears ; two bulls on a mound and two steers on a ridge were they at that time."

There is a vigorous description of a general conflict in the Fenian saga, the *Cath Finn-trágha*, in some respects one of the finest, though not one of the most ancient of our historic-romantic tales. The following is a close translation of portion of it :—

" Thereafter those two equally eager and equally keen armies poured forth against each other, like dense woods, with their proud noisy strokes, and spilling a black deluge, actively, fiercely, perilously, angrily, furiously, destructively, boldly, vehemently, hastily ; and great was the grating of swords against bones, and the cracking of bones that were crushed, and bodies that were mangled, and eyes that were blinded, and arms that were shortened to the back, and mother without son, and fair wife without mate. Then the beings of the upper regions re-sponded to the battle, telling the evil and the woe that was destined to be done on that day, and the sea chattered telling the losses, and the waves raised a heavy woeful great moan in wailing them, and the beasts howled telling of them in their bestial way, and the rough hills creaked with the danger of that attack, and the woods trembled in wailing the heroes, and the grey stones cried from the deeds of the champions, and the winds sighed telling the high deeds, and the earth trembled prophesying the heavy slaughter, and the sun was covered with a blue mantle from the cries of the grey hosts, and the clouds were shining black at the time of that hour, and the hounds and whelps, and crows, and the demoniac women of the glen, and the spectres of the air, and the wolves of the forest howled together from every quarter and every corner round about them, and a demoniacal devilish section of the race of tempters to evil and wrong kept urging them on against each other."

The description of a field of battle has always been a favourite theme with poets, and many is the example of such a description we have, from the battle-scenes of the Prince of Poets, down to Tennyson's splendid lay, "The Charge of the Light Brigade." But it is no exaggeration to say that no great writer, either in prose or poetry, has succeeded in painting a more *vivid*, a more *realistic* picture of a battle-scene than the pictures of the unknown writers of these passages. It should be noticed that most writers describe only the bright side of a battle : they paint its "pride, pomp and circumstance," but they leave out all mention of its more disagreeable details. Gaelic writers on the contrary, are admirably true to nature : they describe the glory of a battle-field with the greatest enthusiasm, but they also depict its horror. We hear not alone the wild, inspiring slogan and the ringing cheer of victory, but also the agonized shriek of the wounded, and the fearful moan of the dying ; not alone the clang of steel on shield and hauberk, but the thud of the fallen champion, and the crushing of his limbs beneath the rush of feet. I would have no hesitation whatever in placing some of these passages, for realistic effect, beside any passage not merely of Scott, Macaulay, or Tennyson, but of Homer himself. I purposely compare this descriptive prose with the descriptive *poetry* of other nations ; for, though nominally prose, it is, in reality, poetry. It may be accurately described as poetical prose, or prose-poetry.

The Gael being notoriously a non-seafaring race, it is rather striking that one of the great fortes of Gaelic writers should lie in the description of the changing moods of the ocean. This remarkable circumstance is probably to be explained by that innate love of nature which is so peculiarly Celtic. Everyone must have noticed how in the extracts I have read the Celtic nature-love, and the Celtic belief in nature's influence over, and sympathy with, man so frequently appear. Almost all the similes of a Gaelic writer are drawn from nature, and particularly from the phenomena connected with the ocean. In the "Battle of Moyrath," for instance, we are told that on the conveying of certain news to him "the stern steadfast heart of Conall started from the mid-upper part of his chest like the noise of a sea-green wave against the earth." In the "Battle of Ventry," it is said of two warriors as they fought that one would think that the "bank overflowing, white-foaming curled wave of Cliodhna, and the long-sided steady wave of Tuagh, and the great right-courageous wave of Rudhraighe had arisen to smother one another." In the "Battle of Rosnaree" the march to battle of the men of Ulster is described as "like the tide of a strong torrent belching through the top of a rugged mountain, so that it bruises and breaks what there is of stones and of trees before it." In the "Pursuit of the *Giolla Deacair*" Diarmuid's rush on his foes "under them, over them, and through them" is compared to that of "hawk through flight of small birds, or wolf through sheep-flock," or to "the weighty rush of a mad swollen stream in spate that over and adown a cliff of ocean spouts."

When we consider this intense love of nature which characterizes the Celt, we cannot wonder that Gaelic writers should especially delight in describing a thing so vast, so powerful, and so mysterious as the ocean. Here is Mr. O'Grady's translation of the description in *Tadhg Mac Céin* of the sailing of Tadhg and his companions :—

"Forth on the vast illimitable abyss they drive their vessel accordingly over the volume of the potent and tremendous deluge, till at last neither ahead of them nor astern could they see land at all, but only colossal ocean's superfices. Further on they heard about them concert of multifarious unknown birds, and hoarse booming of the main ; salmons irridescent, white-bellied, throwing themselves all around the *currach;* in their wake, huge bull-seals thick and dark, that ever cleft the flashing wash of the oars as they pursued them, and following these again great whales of the deep. So that for the prodigiousness of their motion, fashion, and variety, the young men found it a festive thing to scrutinize and watch them all, for hitherto they had not used to see the diverse oceanic reptiles, the bulky marine monsters."

Here is a description of a storm, taken from the *Cath Finntrágha* :—

"Then arose the winds, and grew high the waves, so that they heard nothing but the furious mad sporting of the mermaids, and the many crazy voices of the hovering terrified birds above the pure green waters that were in uproar. There was no welcome forsooth, to him who got the service and attendance of that angry, cold, and deep sea, with the force of the waves, and of the tide, and of the strong blasts; nor was the babbling of those watery tribes pleasant with the creaking of the ropes that were lashed into strings, and with the buffeting of the masts by the fierce winds that shivered them severely."

The extraordinary fertility of language displayed in all these descriptive passages is one of their chief characteristics. Gaelic writers delight in heaping up epithet on epithet, comparison on comparison. These epithets and comparisons exhibit the greatest boldness and vigour, and sometimes they almost startle one with their peculiar vehemence ; but they are always, above all things, appropriate, and convey to the reader's mind a most vivid—in some cases an almost too vivid—picture of what the author is describing. These writers have all a vast range of vocabulary, and it is no uncommon thing to find twenty or thirty adjectives, all of different meaning, but all most applicable, qualifying the same noun. These strings of adjectives are introduced chiefly for the sake of alliteration, which is as prominent a feature of Gaelic prose as it is of Gaelic poetry. All the passages I have quoted are, in the original Irish, full of alliteration and similar effects. Now, this brings home two facts to us : first, the extraordinary plasticity of the language which allows all this, and, secondly, the prodigious amount of labour and pains which must have been bestowed by the authors on these passages.*

---

* The labour required to produce an effective alliterative passage in Irish is, however, by no means so great as we might imagine. Modern English, as everyone knows, does not at all lend itself to alliteration with the facility of Irish. When we attempt to form a continuous alliterative sentence in English we almost always produce nonsense of the "four fat friars fanning fainting flies" type. The genius of Irish, on the contrary, peculiarly fits it for alliteration. I have frequently heard Irish speakers produce fine alliterative sentences quite unconsciously, and we know that Gaelic poets, even of the second or third rank, can dash off alliterative stanzas extemporarily.

Gaelic prose-works are emphatically, and in the fullest sense of the words, works of art,—art the most wonderful, the most consummate and the most finished.

Whilst admiring these alliterative "runs" and descriptive passages, as such, we cannot but admit that their perpetual recurrence is an abuse. The inflated style which marks our romantic tales from the twelfth century onwards stands alone in literature. It is not found in our oldest romances, and there is nothing like it, as far as I am aware, in any other European literature. How it was introduced into Gaelic prose is, however, by no means difficult to conceive. We must never forget that our prose epics were originally intended not to be written, but to be *recited*. The bards, of course, did not learn them off *in extenso ;* indeed no human being— not even an Irish bard—could possibly learn by heart three hundred and fifty prose tales of such length as the great majority of our romances. In all probability the bard learned only the *outline* or *skeleton* of each story, and this outline he filled in extemporarily with his own words whilst in the act of reciting. We can easily conceive how a bard possessing an enormous command over language would revel in rolling forth to his astonished hearers a long list of alliterative adjectives and compound words. Afterwards, when the tales came to be written down, this turgid style was not unnaturally retained ; and succeeding writers imitated, and even outdid the extravagance of the bardic language. This is why the later romance is the more turgid and ornamental, as a rule, in its style. Any attempt to revive this inflated style in modern Irish prose would, of course, be absurd. Such a sentence, for instance, as

" Wrathful, horrid, wrathful-gloomy, ungentle, very-angry, unfriendly, was the keen, angry, very-fiery look that each of them cast on the other from the flashing of the intent-ruinous eyes, under the soft brinks of the frowning, wrinkled cluster-brows " (which occurs in the *Cath Rois na Riogh,*) might be very effective when thundered forth by a bard to an audience of chiefs and gallowglasses, but in a modern composition it would be intolerable.

When this fondness for adjectival ornamentation is kept in restraint nothing can surpass our mediæval romantic tales in simple dignity of style. All the declamation on earth would fail to produce the touching effect of the old story-teller's description of the death of the children of Tuireann * :—

" When Brian heard that he went back to where his two brothers were, and he lay down between them ; and his soul went forth from him and from his two brothers at the same time."

Equally touching is the death of Tuireann himself :—

" After that lay, Tuireann fell on his children, and his soul went from him ; and they were buried immediately in the same grave."

For simplicity and pathos I have never read a passage equal to these, unless, perhaps, it be the description of the death of Diarmuid in the " Pursuit of Diarmuid and Gráinne."

The *purely* fictitious prose tales found in our manuscripts are almost always of a humorous nature. Commenting on this Comáp ó ꝶlanngaile has the following very trenchant remarks :—

" It has been sometimes asserted—by those who

---

* The chaste simplicity which distinguishes the " Fate of the Children of Tuireann " is admirably preserved throughout Mr. O'Duffy's translation.

knew nothing about the subject—that the ancient
and mediæval Irish *had no humour!* the inference
being, we suppose, that we only acquired that
faculty after we had been brought into close connection with the intensely humorous English people,
and had learned their language—the doings of that
people in Ireland during the last three hundred
years being especially humorous and playful, and
so highly adapted to develop in us a playful and
light-hearted disposition! As a matter of fact,
however, half of the modern so-called 'Irish humour'
is nothing but a caricature of the Irishman's manners
or a burlesque of his English dialect. Unfortunately,
it is not Englishmen only who find such things
immensely funny—many of our own countrymen,
too, consider them prime subjects for ridicule.
The more English some of us are the more we think
we are entitled to make game of those who are less
English but more Irish ; for your Cork man laughs
at the Kerry man, the Carlow man at the Cork man,
the Dublin man at the Carlow man, and the Saxon
at us all."

As a specimen of genuine Gaelic humorous
prose Mr. O'Flannghaile quotes a tale from the
introduction to *Silva Gadelica;* it is translated
from an Irish manuscript in the British Museum :

"Three penitents resolved to quit the world for
the ascetic life, and so sought the wilderness. After
exactly a year's silence the first said, ' 'Tis a good
life we lead.' At the next year's end the second
answered, ' It is so.' Another year being run out,
the third exclaimed, ' If I cannot have peace and
quiet here I'll go back to the world ! ' "

A Munster folk-tale very similar to this is
quoted by Mr. O'Flannghaile from the *Gaelic
Journal* for August, 1894 :—

"The hero of it was *Micheal na Buile,* ' Michael
of the Madness,' or ' Mad Mick.' Now, there is a
beautiful valley in Kerry, some miles to the West
of Tralee, and it is called ' *Gleann na nGealt,*'
or ' Madmen's Glen,' and thither the crazy used to

resort to drink its wholesome waters and to eat its cresses. So Mad Mick went to try the waters and the cresses, and to get rest for his poor head. One day a stray cow found her way into the glen, and her lowing might be heard for miles around, but though the glen was full of madmen no one spoke. But at the end of seven years, an old man more acute of hearing than the rest cries out, 'Is that a cow I heard?' Seven years after this a young man answering cries, 'Where did you hear her?' And now, at the end of another seven years, Mick, unable to stand the noisy conversation any longer, cried out, 'The glen is bothered with ye!' And then Mad Mick quitted *Gleann na nGealt*, bothered entirely with the noise and brawling of that same glen."

The powers of description to which I have alluded in connection with the heroic tales are quite as evident in the humorous ones. The following, for example, is Mr. O'Grady's translation of the description of the *Giolla Deacair* and his steed. Owing to the translator's mannerisms it is not, perhaps, quite so racy as it might be.*

---

* Mr. O'Grady constantly goes out of his way to find some odd-looking English word or phrase to translate a quite simple Irish expression. "*Buailios do phreib é,*" for instance, he renders, "*impinges* upon him with a kick;" "*ocus do bhrised cos eich eile,*" he elaborately translates, "and yet another's legs would fracture with a kick." This stilted style of translation is calculated to give the barbarian quite a false notion of Irish prose. There is, however, no doubt about the fact that "*Silva Gadelica*" is one of the monumental books of the century. In his "ᴄeanᵹa ᴄhíopaṁuil na hᴇipeann," Mr. O'Neill Russell expresses the regret that the language of the tales is not easier to be understood by those who have not had opportunity and time to study our older literature. This is scarcely to the point, for Mr. O'Grady's object in " *Silva Gadelica* " is to give some idea, not of modern, but of *mediæval* Irish prose. And, after all, the language of the tales is not so very difficult; an ordinary reader of Irish can certainly understand it as easily as an ordinary reader of English can understand the language of the *Faerie Queene.*

B

A Fiann had been placed on guard by Fionn:—

"Nor had he been long so when out of the
eastern *airt* directly he marked draw towards him
a ruffian, virile indeed, but right ugly, a creature
devilish and misshapen, a grumpy-looking and ill-
favoured loon, equipped as thus : a shield that on
the convex was black and loathly-coloured, gloomy,
hung on his back's expanse ; upon his dingy, grimy
left thigh, all distorted, was a wide-grooved and
clean-striking sword ; stuck up his shoulder he had
two long javelins, broad in the head, which, for a
length of time before, he had not raised in fight or
melée ; over his armature and harness was thrown
a mantle of a limp texture, whilst every limb of
him was blacker than a smith's coal quenched in
cold ice-water. A sulky, cross-built horse was there,
gaunt in the carcase, with skimpy, grey hind-
quarters shambling upon weedy legs, and wearing
a rude iron halter. This beast his master towed
behind him, and how he failed to drag the head
from the neck, and this from the attenuated body,
was a wonder, such plucks he communicated to the
rusty iron halter, and sought thus to knock some
travel or progression out of his nag. But a greater
marvel yet than this it was that the latter missed
of wrenching from his owner's corporal barrel the
thick, long arms of the big man : such the sudden
stands and stops he made against him, and the
jibbing. In the meantime, even as the thunder of
some vast, mighty surf was the resonance of each
ponderously lusty, vigorous whack, that, with an
iron cudgel, the big man laid well into the horse,
endeavouring, as we have said, thus to get some
travel or progression out of him."

This strange cavalier came to the presence of
Fionn, and, after some altercation with Conán
Maol, or "Bald Conán," he asked and obtained
leave to let his horse loose. "The big man,"
pursues the storyteller, "pulls the rough iron
halter which was round the horse's head, and
the creature started off, rushing with mighty
swift strides till it reached the Fianna's horse-

troop," which, it seems, "he began to lacerate
and kill promptly; with a bite he would whip
out the eye of one of them, with a snap he
would snip off the ear of a second, and yet
another's legs would fracture with a kick." The
Fianna, of course, were scarcely disposed to
stand this. "Take thy horse out of that, O
big man!" cried Conán. "1 swear by the
divisions of heaven and earth that, had it not
been on the security of Fionn and the Fianna
thou hast let him free, I would dash his brains
out." "I swear by the divisions of heaven
and earth," said the big man, "that take him
out of that I never will." Conán himself then
succeeded in recapturing the animal, and, on
Fionn's advice, he mounted him in order to
gallop him to death over hills and hollows.
But, in spite of all Conán's endeavours, the
animal obstinately refused to stir. Fionn was
thereupon struck with the idea that it would be
necessary to place on the steed's back the
number of men that would weigh exactly as
much as his master. So no less than thirteen
men mounted behind Conán, and the horse,
curiously enough, lay down under them and
got up again. The *Giolla Deacair*, not relishing
the treatment his faithful nag received, after reciting a lay to Fionn, "weakly and wearily"
departed ; but when he had reached the top of
a hill, he girt up his coat tails, "and away with
him with the speed of a swallow or a roe-deer,
or like a vociferous March wind on the ridge of
a mountain." When the horse saw this, he
immediately started after his master, with Conán
and the thirteen men on his back. Fionn and
the Fianna "guffawed with a shout of mockery
flouting Conán," who "screamed and screeched
for help." Ultimately, however, the Fianna

deemed it advisable to start in pursuit, and they followed the steed over hill and glen till they reached the sea ; here, one of them succeeded in catching the steed by the tail, but he, Conán, and the thirteen men were dragged into the sea, and the Fianna had to pass through many a marvellous adventure before they recovered them again.   I would advise everyone that possibly can to read this truly splendid tale in the original.

In these stories we find, as the critic already quoted says, "the true Irish extravagance, the true Irish love of the incongruous,—the genuine article, independent of brogue or burlesque." It is in this love of the fantastic, or incongruous, that Celtic humour peculiarly consists.   The Celt is famous throughout the world for his wit ; but it is in humour that he is pre-eminent.   And Celtic humour, be it remarked, though sometimes broad enough, is, as a rule, of an exceedingly subtle and delicate kind, so that it is not everyone who can appreciate it.

What an extraordinary and melancholy fact it is that we do not know the authors of any of the works we have been considering.   They exist, splendid, beautiful, and unique ; they have come down to us, almost the only thing that remains of our glorious past ; but the oft-repeated question " Who wrote them ? " is a question no man can answer.   Powerful and judicious must have been the minds that conceived these grand old tales, skilful must have been the hands that wrote them.   But their authors have long since been mouldering in the quiet obscurity of ruined abbeys, and history records not their names. These men wrote not for gain, they wrote not even for the nobler reward of glory, but they wrote out of pure and spontaneous love for literature itself.   What a mighty race they were, those Gaelic bards of old! Honour to their memory! Oblivion has hitherto been their portion; but they have one consolation, for, though their names have been forgotten, their works, which are their second and greater selves, will live on through the ages.

I had intended, Mr. Chairman, to make a few remarks on the works and style of the more modern writers of Gaelic prose, especially of Brother Michael O'Clery and of Geoffrey Keating. At the end of a paper like this, however, I would not have time to do them justice, and consequently shall not attempt to do so. I need only remark that to the ordinary reader, who reads for amusement rather than for instruction, modern Gaelic prose is by no means so interesting as mediæval; whilst it is not nearly so extensive. This is easily explained. The several conquests and re-conquests of Ireland, from the time of the Reformation to that of the Revolution, completely swept away the old order of things. Defeat, conquest, and persecution did not, indeed, silence the Gaelic muse, for we know that much of our sweetest Gaelic poetry was written, or rather composed, for some of it has never been written, during the seventeenth and following centuries; but with prose the case was naturally very different. A good education, leisure, access to libraries, are necessary for the composition of great prose, works; and these were not to be had. When the power of the native chieftains had been broken, and the monasteries had been swept away by the Reformation, the occupation and the *raison d' être* of the bard were gone; and so that noble line of storytellers, that had been held in honour by the Gael for two thousand years, disappeared from the land.

A few words should certainly be said about Irish prose, as written at the present day. Of course, the work that modern Gaelic scholars are engaged in doing is mainly one of revival ; it consists, for the most part, not in original work, but in editing, translating, and annotating existing texts. There is growing up, however, in the ranks of the Gaelic League, a school of modern Gaelic writers ; and their work may be seen, month by month, in the columns of the *Gaelic Journal*. A modern Gaelic prose style is being formed, and, when developed, it will combine, let us hope, the purity and elegance of Keating, with the nature-love and imagination-play of the mediæval romances.

In conclusion, Mr. Chairman, it may be asked what are the future prospects of Gaelic prose literature ? Is this glorious literature a thing of the past ?—a thing on which we may look back with pride indeed, but which is now utterly and irretrievably gone ? Or, can it be that it yet has a future before it ?—that the day will yet come when the bard and the *seanchaidh* will once more hold an honoured place in Eire, when the world will listen in amazement, as it did of yore, to the immortal *sgéalta* of the Gaelic race ? Personally, Mr. Chairman, I am convinced that this day will come ; and that it will come is the firm belief of thousands to-day. We will be met, of course, with the stereotyped objection that the men who say and think these things are enthusiasts ; this is, perhaps, true ; but it would be well to recollect that every great movement that has ever been carried out on this earth has been carried out simply and solely by enthusiasts.

Centuries ago, when the European civilization and literature of to-day were unknown, Eire had her day of empire ; but hers was the empire, not of brute force, but of intellectuality.   Time was when this land of ours was the literary centre of Christendom, when the learned of the world found their chief reading in these very prose tales that we have been considering. Gaelic literature, like the Gaelic race, has long been dying, but it is " fated not to die."   When we remember the past, and when we look into the future, we are driven to admit, laying all enthusiasm aside, or, at least, avoiding extravagance in our enthusiasm, that in centuries yet to come these self-same old epics, these self-same old *sgéalta*, with their simple and beautiful imagery, with their grand and sonorous descriptive passages, with their strange old-world Celtic eloquence, may still be inspiring and rejuvenating the heart of man, and lifting him to higher and nobler ideals.

II.—THE FOLK-SONGS OF IRELAND*

HAVE called this paper "The Folk-Songs of Ireland," Mr. Chairman, simply because I was unable to think of any better title. I fear, however, that the name is calculated to give a false impression of what I really intend to do. Even had I had full materials at hand, which unfortunately, I had not, it would be impossible, within the limits of a paper like this, to treat in anything like an adequate manner a subject so vast and so important as the folk-songs of Ireland. I do not propose, then, to trace in detail, the history of the folk-song,

---

* Read in January, '98. In its original form this paper was considerably longer, as I quoted in full many of the best examples of living Gaelic folk-songs. As most of these, however, are to be found in Dr. Hyde's "Αϐράιn Ϧράϯ Chúιϧe Connαϲϲ," it is unnecessary to print them here. I would advise anyone whom the somewhat desultory remarks contained in the following paper may succeed in interesting in the subject to fly at once to the pages of Dr. Hyde.

entering into an elaborate discussion as to its origin and antiquity ; nor do I propose to make an exhaustive classification and analysis of the Gaelic folk-songs existing at the present day. Such a task would, indeed, be quite beyond me; and I shall have to content myself with making a few rapid and tentative remarks, of a more or less general nature, in the hope of interesting the members of the Society in a species of un-written literature—the expression, though a bull, may be allowed on account of its handiness— which may not, perhaps, up to the present, have received from us that attention which it deserves.

It is in the highest degree probable that every form of literature which we have at the present day has sprung from the folk-tale and the folk-song. These two were, to a by-gone age, all that the press, the novel, and the drama are to ours. Co-æval with man himself, they are, so to speak, the two elemental forms of literature. It is impossible to conceive a state of society in which they did not exist : since man first trod this earth to the present moment, he has loved to wander in the land of fancy opened up by the folk-tale, and to pour forth in song the emotions of his soul.

Most of our great authorities incline to the belief that the folk-tale originated in an attempt on the part of primitive man to bring home more strongly to himself, or, as one might put it, to represent pictorially to himself, the phenomena of nature. The folk-song also, I conceive, owes its existence to the influence of nature on man. We moderns, who live in an atmosphere which we studiously endeavour to render as unnatural as possible, can scarcely form an idea of what nature means to the savage—and the savage, let

us remember, is the man as God made him.
Living in constant contact and communication
with nature, its beauties and potencies stir him
with feelings unknown to us.   Nature is all in
all to him—his friend, his life, his god.   Hence,
just as primitive man attempted, in the folk-tale,
to allegorize in a simple form the phenomena
and objects of nature—representing the cloud
as the boat that sails over land and sea, the sun
as the giant that drinks up lakes and strands fish
and boats, the rainbow as the man that jumps
a hundred miles, the blade of grass as a " slender,
green man"—so, in the folk-song, did he endeavour to give expression to the bounding joy
of his heart at the glorious sounds and sights of
nature—the delight with which he listened to
the bird-song, the mystic fascination with which
he heard the wind-moan, and the streamlet-
laugh, the awe with which he gazed on the
mighty sea and the sombre mountain.   The
song, then, was originally man's hymn of praise
to nature, and, through nature, to God.

If this theory be true we should expect to find
that the earliest songs of every nation are nature-
hymns.   This is exactly what we do find.   The
songs of those nations which are to-day in a
state somewhat similar to that of our ancestors
three thousand years ago, are all expressions
either of praise or of fear, to the forces of nature,
these being very frequently represented as divini-
ties.   The earliest songs of our own race have,
of course, been lost, or, at least, have come down
to us in forms which it is now impossible to re-
cognize.   But going back as far as we possibly
can, we discover that the oldest lines of poetry
extant in any vernacular European tongue, with
the exception of Greek, are those three strange
but beautiful pieces attributed to Amergin, son

of Milidh—traditionally represented as the first
verses ever sung in Eire. Here is how Dr.
Sigerson translates the first few lines of Amergin's " Triumph-Song " :—

"I, the Wind at sea,
I, the roaring Billow,
I, the roar of Ocean,
I, the seven Cohorts,
I, the Ox upholding,
I, the rock-borne Osprey,
I, the flash of Lightning,
I, the Ray in Mazes."

" This poem," says Dr. Hyde, " is noticeable
for its curious pantheistic strain which reminds
one strangely of the East." Pantheistic or not,
it is instinct with the nature-spirit so characteristic of the early productions of every race. I
quote it not, of course, as a folk-song, but as an
instance of the part in which nature-worship has
played in the genesis of Gaelic poetry.

It may be urged by those who are acquainted
with the Gaelic folk-songs of the present day
that comparatively few of them can be described
as nature songs. This is, no doubt, true. We
rarely find a Donegal fisherman singing an
" Ode to the West Wind," or a Connemara
labourer, an " Address to the Daisy." But, is
it not quite possible that many songs which are
now love-songs pure and simple were once
nature-songs ? The folk-memory is, as everyone
knows, wonderfully retentive and conservative.
Yet, we find that, while a folk-tale itself may be
preserved for two thousand years—and preserved
without any radical change in incidents or detail
even to the very word-formulæ and nonsense-
ending—yet the origin and meaning of the tale
have been forgotten. The Mayo peasant, for
instance, who relates the story of Páidín drink-

ing up the lake,* no more dreams that Páidín is, in all probability, a solar-myth, than he does that his own grandfather sleeping in the church-yard hard-by is one.   In the same way, whilst the ideas and words of a folk-song may be preserved, its meaning and origin may, in many cases, have been completely lost.

In quite recent times we find a striking example of such a process,—a case in which the meaning and origin, not of a single song, but of a whole class of songs, have been forgotten, though the songs themselves, which include some of the finest in the language, are popular all over Gaelic-speaking Ireland to-day.   The eighteenth century poets almost always referred to Ireland under some allegorical name,—and very beautiful these allegorical names are. "Róirín Ðuḃ," "Siġle Ní Ṡaṁra," "Caicilín Ní Uallaċáin,"—these and many more were originally patriotic or political songs, but are now sung as love-songs.   The "Páircín Fionn," too, is considered by Hardiman to represent the son of James II.—thus forming one of the most remarkable instances on record of a song's having lost its meaning, the "Páircín Fionn" being now treated as a *girl*.   What has happened in the case of this particular class of song may very well have happened in the case of many more.

It is true, of course, that most of the Gaelic folk-songs current to-day, are, in their present forms at least, not more than one or two centuries old.   But the antiquity of existing folk-songs is often much greater than would at first sight appear.   We may, for instance, come

---

* See "*An Sgeuluidhe Gaodhalach*," *Cuid I.*

across a Munster song, which, from its language
and style, and from the political or other allusions which it may contain, we may be inclined
to set down as, say, one hundred and fifty years
old. We may then fall in with a Connacht
version of the same song, and soon after with an
Ulster version, both of about the same date as
the Munster song. Now, when we find three
distinct versions of a folk-song, each belonging
to a different province, and the three of ap-
proximately the same date, we must necessarily
conclude that all three versions have come
from a common root,—a folk-song, that is,
belonging to some date at least a century or two
earlier than that of the three existing versions.
We thus see that the language of a folk-song
forms a very far from infallible guide to its
antiquity ; and it is quite possible that many of
our best-known and most modern-looking songs
are some centuries older than they appear.

Further than this, however, it is highly probable that there exist a small number of folk-
songs which are of the very highest antiquity.
We know that the greater number of our
folk-tales are of comparatively modern date, —
either accounts, more or less embellished with
imagination, of events which have actually
occurred among the peasantry, or else pure
and simple inventions of the folk-fancy ; but
we know also that there are a number of old
tales,—including those which contain traces of
nature-myths,—which have been handed down
by word of mouth for two or three thousand
years. Now, there is no reason in the world
that what is true of the folk-tale should not also
be true of the folk-song. Most of those current
to-day are, as has been said, of comparatively
recent date ; but, reasoning from analogy,

nothing is more probable than that there is many a folk-song sung to-day around the turf-fire of a Munster cabin, or on the bare side of a Connacht mountain, which has been sung by generation after generation since the Gael first set foot in Eire.

Let us turn, however, from dry theorizing to the warm living folk-songs themselves.   Here, at any rate, we are on firm ground.   The question of their age and origin, interesting as it undoubtedly is, is, after all, but of secondary importance : be they centuries old, or be they but of yesterday, they are here, and they speak for themselves.   Had the Gaelic race never produced a scrap of literature—had our treasures of history and romance never had a being, had our Cormacs, and our O'Clerys, and our Keatings, and our Donnchadh Ruadhs, never written a line—these folk-songs of ours would still have been sufficient to prove for all time the glorious capabilities of our race.   Let the scoffer scoff as he wills—let the up-to-date young Irishman fresh from the " National' School, or from the still worse, and still more un-Irish Intermediate *regime,* sneer as he, and he only, *can* sneer, let him solace his soul with the London music-hall song, and the pantomime ballad—but the fact remains that these folk-songs exist, the fact remains that the brains of Irish-speaking peasant men and women have given birth to them, the fact remains that, by wilfully making up his mind to ignore them, and their language, he is committing an act, not merely of egregious folly, but of actual criminality, for which his children and his children's children may curse him yet.

In his folk-songs the Gaelic peasant reveals himself in a new light to us.   He shows us a

side of his character hitherto unknown and un-
dreamt of. We behold him wandering in an ideal
world of his own. Black, dreary bog ; damp, half-
roofless mud-cabin—these things are forgotten.
He shows himself the poet and the dreamer
now as of yore. We hear him pouring out, in
his folk-songs, his feelings of joy or of sorrow, of
love or of hate. We hear the peasant-girl singing by her spinning-wheel, hear the mother
crooning over her infant, hear the lover giving
utterance, in sweet and passionate language, to
the love which fills his soul. The rollicking
strain of the drinking-song mingles with the sad
piercing note of the *caoineadh*,— the plaintive
wail of the young mother carried off by the
sluagh-sidhe mingles with the hymn of love and
trust to the *Muire Máthair*. Love, and joy, and
sorrow, and hope,—these are the notes that
perpetually ring through our folk-poetry, as
through our folk-music,—these are the tints that
colour the lives and character of our people.

The Gaelic folk-song, be it remembered, is
totally distinct, not only from the technical
poetry of the ancient bards, but also from the
highly-polished, voluptuous, and, as it has been
well called, Swinburne-like poetry of the 18th
century Munster school. The folk-song proper
is the product of a folk-poet, and the common
possession of the folk-people. Hence, it possesses those two distinguishing characteristics of
the folk-fancy—simplicity of language and beauty
of thought.

Simplicity, beautiful and almost childlike
simplicity, both of idea and language—this is,
above all things, the leading characteristic of
Gaelic folk-poetry, as, indeed, of all folk-poetry.
The ideas are such as a child might grasp, the
language such as a child might use and under-

stand. Take, for instance, such a song as
"Θιbℓín a Rúin," probably the best known and
most popular in the language. Is it possible to
conceive anything more beautifully simple than
the poet-lover's declaration ?—

> "'Oo ŕιubaℓŕaınn an ŕaoξaℓ móŕ ℓeac,
> Αὲc cℓeaṁnaŕ o' ŕaξáıℓ ó'm ŕcóŕ,
> '8 ní ŕcaŕŕaınn ξo oeó ℓeacŕa,
> Α Θιbℓín a ŕúın ! "

Or his bold impassioned question :—

> " Α' octocŕaιò nó'n bŕanŕaιò cú,
> Α Θιbℓín a ŕúın ? "

Or Eibhlín's answer :—

> " Cιocŕaιò mé 'ŕ ní ŕanŕaιò mé,
> Cιocŕaιò mé 'ŕ ní ŕanŕaιò mé,
> Cιocŕaιò mé 'ŕ ní ŕanŕaιò mé,
> '8 euℓoξaιò mé ℓe m' ŕcóŕ ! "

Take again, say, the "Páıŕcín Fıonn." For
beautiful and simple effect what could surpass
either version of its chorus ? —either that beginning :—

> "1ŕ cuŕa mo ŕún, mo ŕún, mo ŕún,"

Or that other version, which commences :—

> '8 óŕó, boξ ℓıomŕa, boξ ℓıomŕa, boξ ℓıomŕa."

Assuredly, language is capable of nothing more
inexpressibly soft and melodious than this song.

The extreme simplicity of our folk-songs
extends not merely to the thoughts and language
but also, very naturally, to the metre. The
thought and word parallelism, the intricate
internal assonances, the studious employment
of alliteration, so characteristic of *literary* Irish
poetry—these, as a rule, are absent from the
folk-song. The verse-structure is of the simplest
imaginable kind. Here, for instance, is the
opening stanza of a song in which a peasant-girl
caoines for her absent lover :—

" Mo ḃrón aр an ḃraiррġe,
1ṛ ó aċá móр,
1ṛ ó ġaḃáil ιοιр mé,
'8 mo ṁíle ṛtóр ! "

Dr. Hyde's English version of this stanza runs:—

" My grief on the sea,
How the waves of it roll !
For they heave between me
And the love of my soul !"

The language and ideas throughout this song are so simple that we may well believe it was the composition of a peasant-woman. Dr. Hyde got it from an old woman named Ḃрιġιο Ní Coррuaιḋ (anglicé, Biddy Crummey), who lived in a hut in the middle of a bog in Roscommon. As he mournfully remarks, "Cá рí maрḃ anoιṛ 7 a cuιο aḃрán leιte," "She is dead now, and her songs with her."

One of the chief charms of the folk-imagination is the originality, the quaintness, the oddness of its conception. What could be more delightfully quaint and original than the song composed by the fairies of Knockgraffon, aided by the little hunchback Lusmore ? Or, to take a very different example, than that beautiful dialogue, "Caòġ aġuр Máιре," one of the finest songs in the language ?

It is a remarkable fact that our folk-poetry contains so iittle of a ballad nature. Love-songs we have, and drinking-songs, and occupation-songs, and lullabies, and *caoineadhs*,—but few songs, if any, which contain a regular story. The nearest approach, perhaps, is in a certain class of religious songs, many of them in the form of a dialogue between Death and a Sinner, or Death and a Lady, perhaps, or Death and Someone-else,—long and uninteresting enough frequently, to tell the truth. The best example of this kind of religious ballad I have ever come across is a really fine poem called " The Keening of the Three Marys," which, with a poetical translation, will be found in Dr. Hyde's " Οὖράιη Ὀιαὁα Chúιɠe Connaċτ."

Fond as they are of story-telling, the ballad seems to have little attraction for our folk-people. What they delight in, above everything else, is their love-songs ; and accordingly we find that their love-songs are not only the most numerous but also, as a rule, by far the best intrinsically. It is in the love-song that the folk-poet shows best the beauty, and wealth, and originality of his imagination, the depth and tenderness of his soul. The love-song, indeed, is the form in which all the grandest and most poetical aspirations of our nature find expression. Next to love of God and love of country, love of woman is the noblest feeling that can stir men's souls ; and well did our Gaelic folk-poets feel this, for they have left us many of the most beautiful and most valuable love-songs in the world.

I have already referred to that wonderful beauty of thought which characterises our folk-songs. What a lovely expression, for instance, is " ρéαὶτ eoὶαιρ," " star of knowledge," or " guiding-star," and how appropriately it is applied by a lover to the one he loves. Another star-comparison—more beautiful still, perhaps— is " ρéαὶτan τρίο an ɠceó," " a star through the mist." A girl says to her lover :—

> " Οὖ óɠánaiɡ óiɠ maρ ρéαὶτan τρίο an ɠceó,
> Ὀo τuɠaρ·ρα mo ɠean ɠo ὶéiρ ὁuιτ,"

which Dr. Hyde translates :—

> " Oh ! youth, whom I have kissed like a star through the mist,
> I have given thee this heart altogether."

What a bold and beautiful comparison is that in "Ⲧⲁⲟ̇ᵹ ⲁᵹⲩⲣ Ⲙⲁⲓⲛⲉ" :—

"Ⲃⲁ ⲟ̇ⲩⲓⲃⲉ ⲃⲓ́ ⲁⲛ ᵹⲛⲓⲁⲛ ⲁᵹ ⲗⲩⲓᵹⲉ
ⲓⲟⲛⲁ́ ⲇⲟ ᵹⲛⲩⲓⲛ, ⲁ Ⲙⲏⲁⲓⲛⲉ,"—

" Blacker was the sun at setting than thy face, my Mary ! " or, as Dr. Hyde renders it in the exact metre of the original :—

"The setting sun shows black and dun
And cold beside thee, Mary."

One more example will suffice. Could lovelier or more appropriate similes be found than these ?

"Ⲁ'ⲥ ⸂ⲁⲟⲓⲗ ⲙⲉ́, ⲁ ⲥⲧⲟ́ⲓⲛⲓ́ⲛ,
Ᵹⲟ ⲙⲃⲁ ᵹⲉⲁⲗⲁⲥ̇ ⲁᵹⲩⲣ ᵹⲛⲓⲁⲛ ⲧⲩ,
Ⲁ'ⲥ ⸂ⲁⲟⲓⲗ ⲙⲉ́ 'ⲛⲁ ⲟ̇ⲓⲁⲓᵹ ⲥⲓⲛ
Ᵹⲟ ⲙⲃⲁ ⲥⲛⲉⲁⲥ̇ⲧⲁ ⲁⲛ ⲁⲛ ⲥⲗⲓⲁⲃ̇ ⲧⲩ ;
Ⲁ'ⲥ ⸂ⲁⲟⲓⲗ ⲙⲉ́ 'ⲛⲁ ⲟ̇ⲓⲁⲓⲟ̇ ⲥⲓⲛ
Ᵹⲟ ⲙⲃⲁ ⲗⲟ́ⲥ̇ⲛⲁⲛⲛ ⲟ́ Ⲇ̇ⲏⲓⲁ ⲧⲩ,
Ⲛⲟ́ ᵹⲩⲛ ⲁⲃ ⲧⲩ ⲁⲛ ⲛⲉ́ⲁⲗⲧ-ⲉⲟⲗⲁⲓⲥ,
Ⲁ̇ᵹ ⲇⲩⲗ ⲛⲟ́ⲙ̇ⲁⲙ ⲁ'ⲥ 'ⲙⲟ ⲟ̇ⲓⲁⲓⲟ̇ ⲧⲩ ! "

Dr. Hyde's translation is :—

" I thought, O my love ! you were so—
As the moon is, or sun on a fountain,
And I thought after that you were snow,
The cold snow on top of the mountain ;
And I thought after that you were more,
Like God's lamp shining.to find me,
Or the bright star of knowledge before,
And the star of knowledge behind me ! "

Assuredly the minds which conceived such thoughts and shaped them into such words must have been the minds of true poets. So elevated, so refined, so free from anything approaching coarseness, is the language of these songs that it is almost incredible that their authors were peasant men and women. Yet such is the fact.   Peasant men and women they were, born and bred in the middle of a bog, perchance, or in a mud-cabin on a mountain-side.   Poor they were, the poorest of the poor; ignorant, too, ·if you will—ignorant, that is, of reading and writing, ignorant of the English language ; but POETS they were, poets taught by nature herself.   Someone has said that poetry is the language of the soul.   If this is true, then must our Gaelic folk-poets be poets of the highest order—for their songs come straight from the soul : they are the simple, artless, poetic, out-pourings of the souls of a simple, artless, poetic people.   The folk-poets of our race have left us songs which would do honour to Burns—songs which, considering the circumstances under which they were written, rank, aesthetically, higher than the songs of Burns.

And one great merit the folk-songs of Ireland possess—a merit possessed by the folk-poetry of few nations, a merit possessed by the love-poetry of fewer still.   Even Burns himself, true poet as he was, occasionally introduces into his most beautiful love-songs allusions and com-parisons which shock all fastidious ears.   Never do we find this in our Gaelic folk-songs.   Pure they are and spotless as the driven snow, like the souls and lives of those who sing them; sweet they are as the scent of the wild mountain-flowers which grow in their native homes ; musical they are as the ripple of the streamlet, as the note of the blackbird, as the laugh of a happy and innocent girl ; grand they are and time-honoured as the Gaelic race itself.   May they never die away on the hillside and in the valley, may they continue to be sung by the hearthside of our people for many a day to come.   They are going from us—we feel it, we

see it, we know it ; let us save them ere it be
too late, and it is not too late yet.   Save the
language, and the folk-tale, and the folk-song,
and all the treasures accumulated in the folk-
mind during three thousand years will be saved
also.   The cause is a holy one—God grant it
may succeed !   May our language, and our
literature, and our folk-lore live ; and if they
live, then, too, will our race live "ᵹo bᴘuınn an
bᴘáᴅa."

III.—THE INTELLECTUAL FUTURE OF THE GAEL*

M R. CHAIRMAN, Ladies, and Gentlemen—Though the duties of an Auditor practically begin and end with the delivery of the Inaugural Address, yet the position is, from one point of view, a far from enviable one. Like most posts of honour it is also a post of danger, as on the success or failure of the Inaugural Address depends, to some extent, the success or failure of the Session. The members of the Society have done me the honour of re-electing me to the position of Auditor, and, whilst deeply sensible of this honour, particularly as I know better than anyone how wholly unmerited it is on my part, I cannot but reflect

---

* Delivered as Inaugural Address of the Session, '97-'98 (October, '97).

with misgiving that I run the risk of losing any
little degree of credit I may have gained by my
Inaugural Address last Session.   However, I am
not given to making excuses : if the Address
please you no excuses will be necessary ; and if,
as is more probable, it fail to do so, all the
excuses I could possibly make would not tend
to mend matters in the slightest degree.   I
prefer, then, to trust to your generosity; and I
shall meekly bear whatever criticisms it may
please you to make.

"The Intellectual Future of the Gael" is a
subject which must, from its very nature, be of
the deepest interest to us ; a subject which must
be fascinating not only to men and women of
Gaelic race, but to all who have at heart the
great causes of civilization, education, and
progress ; to all who bow before the "might of
mind," the majesty of intellect ; to all, in short,
who take an interest in the intellectual life of
mankind—and this is, after all, the true life, for
life without intellect is death.   To all these,
then, but especially to us—to us, Irishmen,
young, ardent, enthusiastic, trying to grope amid
the darkness for a path to higher things—no
question can be of more absorbing interest than
this :   What has destiny in store for this ancient
race of ours?   Is our noonday of glory gone by
for ever ?   Or have we still a future before us
more glorious than we have ever dreamt of in our
moments of wildest enthusiasm?   I shall try
this evening, Mr. Chairman, to find an answer
to this question ; and if my ideas on the subject
do not exactly coincide with those to which we
are accustomed, it is because I believe that the
ends which, as a nation, we have hitherto striven
to attain are *ignes fatui* which are fated to elude
us for ever.

Others have been struck before now by the fact that hundreds of noble men and true have fought and bled for the emancipation of the Gaelic race, and yet have all failed.   Surely, if ever cause was worthy of success, it was the cause for which Laurence prayed, for which Hugh of Dungannon planned, for which Hugh Roe and Owen Roe fought, for which Wolfe Tone and Lord Edward and Robert Emmet gave their lives, for which Grattan pleaded, for which Moore and Davis sang, for which O'Connell wore himself out with toil.   Yet these men prayed and planned, and fought and bled, and pleaded and wrote, and toiled in vain.   May it not be that there is some reason for this?   May it not be that the ends they struggled for were ends never intended for the Gael?   Surely, Mr. Chairman, it would seem so.   The Gael is a splendid soldier; yet it is extremely problematic whether we shall ever be a great military nation like Germany or France.   The Gael is, and always has been, a cunning artificer, a subtle mechanic; yet it is almost certain that we shall never be a great manufacturing or commercial nation like England.   Does it not seem that a nobler destiny than either of these awaits us?   We have struggled as no other nation has struggled; we have bled as no other nation has bled; we have endured an agony compared with which the agonies of other nations have been as child's play.   Time after time have we lifted the chalice of victory to our lips; time after time have we essayed to quaff its delicious contents; yet time after time has it been dashed to the ground.   To-day, after a continuous fight lasting for eight long centuries, we are, Heaven knows, farther off than ever from the goal towards which we have struggled.   Who can look at our political and national life at the present moment, and continue to hope? The men whom we call our leaders are engaged in tearing out one another's vitals, and there is no prospect that they will ever stop. The people are listlessly looking on—for the first time in Irish history they seem to be sunk in apathy. We are tempted to cry aloud in our despair, "O God! will the morning *never* come? Yes, the morning *will* come, and its dawn is not far off. But it will be a morning different from the morning we have looked for. The Gael is not like other men; the spade, and the loom, and the sword are not for him. But a destiny more glorious than that of Rome, more glorious than that of Britain awaits him : to become the saviour of idealism in modern intellectual and social life, the regenerator and rejuvenator of the literature of the world, the instructor of the nations, the preacher of the gospel of nature-worship, hero-worship, God-worship—such, Mr. Chairman, is the destiny of the Gael.

Before I proceed to fill in this outline, it may be well if I digress for a few moments, to consider what races have, up to the present, contributed most to the intellectual advancement of mankind. First of all occurs to every mind the name of the Greeks—the pioneers of intellectual progress in Europe. Who can refuse his admiration to the nation which poured forth a stream of fire which to day, after the lapse of three thousand years, is still enlightening and elevating mankind? Mighty changes have passed over the earth during those three thousand years ; but the epic sung so long ago by

" The blind old man of Scio's rocky isle,"

still instructs, and benefits, and delights us. The

c

world's greatest epic poet, the world's greatest
orator, several of the world's greatest lyric poets,
dramatists, and philosophers—these has Greece
given to the human race. Next came the Roman :
but the Roman directed his splendid energies
towards other ends, and, beyond the work accomplished by one or two great men, his influence
on intellectual history has not been great—has
not, by any means, been proportional to what he
might have done.   Amongst modern nations
those which have contributed most to the intellectual welfare of mankind are undoubtedly
Italy, England and Germany.   It is the great
men of these nations along with those of Greece
that have made the literature of the world.

　　But is it not unquestionable that the influence
of these men—the Homers, and Dantes, and
Shakespeares, and Miltons—is gradually growing
less and less ?   Is it not unquestionable also
that, at the present moment no literature is being
produced in Europe, or in the world, worthy of
the name ?   The vigorous minds of the day are
engaged in producing writings which must, from
their nature, be purely emphemeral—criticisms
reviews, magazine articles—things which, however excellent and highly-finished in themselves,
are, as a rule, forgotten as soon as read.   Two
or three writers are making desperate efforts to
achieve fame by selecting the most *outré* and
absolutely startling subjects to write of which
even their prolific brains can devise. Nowadays
no author can hope for popularity unless, like
one popular novelist, he goes to Hell for a hero,
or, like another, he makes a practice of libelling
all that is sacred and sublime under pretence of
zeal for liberty and truth.   One novel has Satan
for its hero, another has God for its villain.

　　Now, this may be modern, and up-to-date,

and all that ; but, I ask, is it pure, good, healthy, natural literature ? Is it literature which tends to exalt the soul, to make us better, holier, happier ? No, Mr. Chairman, emphatically no. The truth of the matter is that the intellectual and literary tastes of the world have been carried away by a craving for the unreal, for the extravagant, for the monstrous, for the immoral. Men's tastes have become vitiated. There is no healthy out-of-door atmosphere in modern literature. Literature has arrived, in short, at a state of unnatural senility, and the time seems not far off when either of two things must happen— either intellect and literature must disappear from modern life, and with them everything that makes life worth living, or some new and unpolluted source must be opened up, some new blood must be infused into the intellectual system of the world, which has become prematurely worn out. Now, whence is this new blood to come ? The answer is plain : there is but one race, among the races of to-day, which possesses a literature natural and uncontaminated ; there is but one race which possesses an intellectual wealth which, though as old as history, is yet young and vigorous and healthy, and has a future before it rich with undeveloped possibilities. Needless to say, Mr. Chairman, this race is the Gaelic race—a race whose literature is as different from the unnatural literature of to-day as the pure radiance of the sun is different from the hideous glare ot the electric light, as the free breath of heaven is different from the stifling atmosphere of a crowded theatre or music-hall.

I have indicated, then, Mr. Chairman, what seems to me to be the true mission of the Gael, and it will be seen that in this mission the creation, or rather the propagation, of a nature-literature plays a most important part. I do not say the *creation* of a nature-literature, for the excellent reason that it has not to be created: as a matter of fact, it already exists, and only wants to be developed, to be matured, to be expanded. Now, this literature is totally different from every other literature in the world, and this is one of the reasons why it proves so entrancing to everyone who makes a study of it. Gaelic literature, we should remember, has grown up among and been developed by the Gael alone. Its sources of inspiration have been entirely native, and in this one point, at least, it can claim superiority even to Greek literature itself. As regards *manner* and *style*, it has been absolutely uninfluenced by the literature of any other nation. This is why it is so unique, so peculiar, so unlike everything else we are accustomed to, so *refreshing*—that is the proper word to apply to it. It has a quaint, old-world magic, and charm, and glamour that mark it as peculiarly fit to accomplish the reformation we have seen to be so necessary.

To give a more accurate idea of the form this reformation is to take, and of its effects, I would draw special attention to two points in the temperament of the Gael: his love for nature, and his veneration for his heroes. The intellectual life and atmosphere of the present day are, as I have said, nothing if not unnatural. The Gael, on the other hand, like all the Celts, is distinguished by an intense and passionate love for nature. The Gael is the high-priest of nature. He loves nature not merely as something grand, and beautiful, and wonderful, but as something possessing a mystic connection with and influence over man. In the cry of

the seagull as he winged his solitary flight over
the Atlantic waves, in the shriek of the eagle as
he wheeled around the heights of the Kerry
Mountains, in the note of the throstle as she
sang her evening lay in the woods of Slieve
Grot, in the roar of the cataract as it foamed
and splashed down the rocky ravine, in the sob
of the ocean as it beat unceasingly against the
cliffs of Achill, in the sigh of the wind as it
moved, ghostlike, through the oaks of Derry-
bawn—in all these sounds the ancient Gael
heard a music unheard by other men, all these
sounds spoke to his inmost heart in whispers
mysterious and but half understood : they spoke
to him as the voices of his ancestors urging him
to be noble and true—as the voices of the
glorious dead calling to him across the waters
from Tír na n-Og.

The Gael believed, too, that the earth, and
the air, and the sea were filled with strange
beings that exerted a mysterious but potent
influence over him. Everyone who has the
slightest acquaintance with Gaelic literature
knows how this belief appears and reappears on
every page ; how the creatures of the upper
air and the beasts of the forest are represented
as sympathizing with the changing fortunes of
men ; how, during a battle, the blackbird wails
in the wood, the sea chatters telling of the
slaughter, the rough hills creak with terror at
the assault ; and how, when anything remarkable occurs, such as the death of a hero, or the
overwhelming of a favourite champion by un-
equal odds, the three great Waves of Eire cry
out—the furious red Wave of Rudhraighe, the
foam-stormy, ship-sinking Wave of Cliodhna,
and the flood-high, bank-swollen Wave of
Tuagh.

Closely connected with, and, indeed, directly dependent on this love of the Gael for nature, is his capacity for worshipping his heroes. Hero-worship, no doubt, is often carried to extremes; we are prone too frequently to mistake the hero for the cause, to place the man before the principle. But there can be no doubt that hero-worship, in its highest form, is a soul-lifting and an ennobling thing. What would the world be without its heroes? Greece without her Hercules and her Achilles, Rome without her Romulus and her Camillus, England without her Arthur and her Richard, Ireland without her Cúchulainn and her Fionn, Christianity without its Loyolas and its Xaviers? And what is true of hero-worship in general is true, in an especial manner, of the hero-worship of the Gael. When great men died the ancient Gael did not believe that they had passed away for ever from human ken—he believed, on the contrary, that their spirits lingered round the lonely hills and glens, round old moss-grown *lioses* and crumbling *dúns*, round the haunted *sidhe-brughs* and fairy *ráths*—he believed that they hovered near their children, watching over them and taking an interest in their every action. Now, when a man believes that the spirits of the mighty dead, the spirits of those he has loved and venerated, are near him and watching over him, he cannot but endeavour to make himself nobler, better, worthier of the great ones who have preceded him.

> " Lives of great men all remind us
> We can make *our* lives sublime,
> And departing leave behind us
> Footprints on the sands of time."

The spirit of these words of the great modern American poet was perfectly understood by the

ancient Gael. Fearghus, Conchubhar, Cúchulainn, Fionn, Oisín, Oscar,—these were more
to the Gael than the mere names of great
champions and warriors of a former time : they
represented to him men who had gone before,
who had fought the good fight, who had passed
from earth to the mystic Tír na n-óg, who had
become gods,—but whose spirits, heroic and
immortal, still lived after them. And though
well-nigh two thousand years have rolled away
since those mighty heroes trod this land of ours,
yet is their spirit not dead : it lives on in our
poetry, in our music, in our language, and,
above all, in the vague longings which we feel
for a something, we know not what,—our irre-
sistible, overmastering conviction that we, as a
nation, are made for higher things. Oh ! that
this hero-spirit were stronger than it is ! Oh !
that men could be brought to realize that
they are MEN, not animals,—that they could be
brought to realize that, though " of the earth,
earthy," yet that there is a spark of divinity
within them ! And men *can* be brought to
realize this by the propagation of a literature
like that of the Gael,—a literature to which
nature-love and hero-love shall form the key-
words, a literature which shall glorify all that is
worthy of glory,—beauty, strength, manhood,
intellect, and religion.

The mission of the Gael, however, will not be
confined merely to the propagation of this
literature. The Gael is, in the fullest sense of
the word, an idealist ; he is, in fact, *the* idealist
amongst the nations. All that is beautiful,
noble, true, or grand will always find in him a
devotee. He revels in imagination. He loves
to gaze on what is beautiful, to listen to sweet
and rapturous sounds. Hence, painting, sculp-

ture, music, oratory, the drama, learning, all
those things which delight and ravish the human
soul, which stir up in it mighty, convulsive
passions, and strange, indefinable yearnings
after the Great Unknown, all those things which
seem, as it were, links between humanity and
Divinity—these will ever find among the Gael
their most ardent and accomplished disciples.
What the Greek was to the ancient world
the Gael will be to the modern ; and in no
point will the parallel prove more true than
in the fervent and noble love of learning which distinguishes both races.   The
Gael, like the Greek, loves learning, and
like the Greek, he loves it solely for its own sake.
For centuries, when it was sought by penal legis-
lation to deprive him of it, when the path to
honour and wealth was closed to him, and when
learning could be of no advantage to him at
least from a worldly point of view, still did he
cling to it.   The spirit which animated our
O'Clerys and our Keatings still animated their
humbler successors.   The hunted priests and
schoolmasters of the seventeenth and eighteenth
centuries carried about with them from cave to
cave, and from glen to glen, not only copies of
the Gospels, but copies of the Greek and Latin
classics, and volumes of old Gaelic poetry,
history, and romance.   Hundreds of young men
are annually turned out of our modern universi-
ties with a classical education far inferior to that
imparted in the hedge-schools of Munster during
the last century.   When love of learning is so
deeply implanted in the heart of the Gael
that not even persecution, penury, and de-
gradation can eradicate it, surely it ought
to blaze forthwith ten-fold brilliancy when the
night is past and the morn is come.   The

dream of the great English cardinal may yet
come true :—

" I contemplate," says John Henry Newman, " a
people which has had a long night and will have an
inevitable day. I am turning my eyes towards a
hundred years to come, and I dimly see the island
I am gazing on become the road of passage between
two hemispheres, and the centre of the world : I
see its inhabitants rival Belgium in populousness,
France in vigour, and Spain in enthusiasm ; and I
see England taught by advancing years to exercise
in its behalf that good sense which is her characteristic towards everyone else. The capital of that
prosperous and hopeful land is situate on a beautiful
bay, and near a romantic region ; and in it I see a
flourishing University.... Thither as to a sacred soil,
the home of their fathers, the fountain-head of their
Christianity, students are flocking from east and
west, and south—from America, from Australia and
India, from Egypt and Asia Minor, with the ease and
rapidity of a locomotion not yet discovered ; and last,
though not least, from England . . . . . all owning
one faith, all eager for one large true wisdom ; and
thence, when their stay is over, going back again to
carry over all the earth ' Peace to men of goodwill.' "

I am aware, Mr. Chairman, that there are
many here who may consider that the picture I
have drawn is a far too rosy one, who may say
that "The Intellectual Future of the Gael " is
an excellent theme on which one may wax
eloquent—is a catchy title, perhaps, for the
Inaugural Address of a Literary Society—but
that, beyond this, the talk about nature-literature,
about hero-love, and the rest, is little more than
the raving of an enthusiast. Well, Mr. Chairman,
I admit that I *am* an enthusiast, and I glory in
being one. To those who would object that the
sketch I have attempted to give of the intellectual
future of our race is a mere ideal picture, I would
reply that it is *intended* as an ideal picture. If

you wish to accomplish anything great place an
ideal before you, and endeavour to live up to
that ideal.

Now, has the Gael been able to attain the
ideals he has hitherto placed before him, or
does it appear likely that he ever will? Assuredly
not. Nothing seems to me so certain, nothing
seems to me so logical a consequence of our
temperament, of our history, of our present circumstances, as that, if we are to have any future,
it must be an intellectual future. And is there
anyone who would not prefer such a future?
It is, no doubt, a glorious thing to rule over
many subject peoples, to dictate laws to far-off
countries, to receive every day cargoes of rich
merchandise from every clime beneath the sun;
but if to do these things we must become a
soulless, intellectual, Godless race—and it
seems that one is the natural and necessary
consequence of the other,—then let us have
none of them. Do the millions that make up
the population of modern nations—the millions
that toil and sweat, from year's end to year's
end, in the mines and factories of England, the
Continent, and the United States—live the life
intended for man? Have they intellect?
Have they soul? Are they conscious of
man's dignity, of man's greatness? Do they
understand the grandeur of living, and breath-
ing, and working out one's destiny on this
beautiful old earth? The sea, with its mighty
thunderings, and its mysterious whisperings, the
blue sky of day, the dark and solemn canopy of
night spangled with its myriad stars, the mountains and hills steeped in the magic of poetry
and romance—what are these things to them?
What are the hero-memories of the past to
them? Are they one whit the better because

great men have lived, and wrought and died ?
Were the destiny of the Gael no higher than
theirs, better for him would it have been, had
he disappeared from the earth centuries ago.

Intellect and soul, a capacity for loving the
beautiful things of nature, a capacity for worship-
ing what is grand and noble in man, these
things we have yet : let us not cast them from
us in the mad rush of modern life. Let us
cherish them, let us cling to them : they have
come down to us through the storms of centuries—the bequest of our hero-sires of old ;
and when we are a power on earth again, we shall
owe our power, not to fame in war, in statesman-
ship, or in commerce, but to those two precious
inheritances, intellect and soul.

Another thousand years will have rolled over
the earth, and the bard, and the *seanchaidh*, and
the teacher of the Gael, will once more be held
in honour. A better, purer, and happier world
will be listening in rapt amazement to the grand
old epics and time-honoured *sgéalta* of our race.
Men's gods will no longer be empire, ambition,
and gold : but the homage that is paid to those
things to-day will be paid in that happy age, as
it was in days of yore, on the hills and in the
valleys of Eire, to the mysterious potencies of
nature, the beauty and virtue of woman, the
heroic dignity of man, the awful and incompre-
hensible majesty of the Divinity. This, Mr.
Chairman, will be the gospel of the future ; and
to preach this gospel—world-old, yet new, so
true, yet so little realized, so beautiful, and so
ennobling—will be the mission of the children of
the Gael.